HOW THE GRINCH STOLE
HOLLYWOOD

THE MAKING OF THE MOVIE
DR. SEUSS' HOW THE GRINCH STOLE CHRISTMAS!

Starring Jim Carrey as the Grinch
by Andy Lipschultz, with an introduction by Ron Howard

RANDOM HOUSE 🏠 NEW YORK

ACKNOWLEDGMENTS:
To all the motion picture artists who created such an amazing world that it even made sense to publish a book. And to those who did the legwork: Nancy Cushing-Jones, Cindy Chang, the Irish consigliere on the 8th floor, Bette Einbinder, Latifa Ouaou, Heidi Holicker, Bill Sturgeon, Bob Hoffman, Scott Shields, and Paul Molles. Most of all to Ron Howard, who really didn't have the time but always found the time.

Photography by Ron Batzdorff, except as follows: Michael Garland: page 42 bottom, page 48 bottom, page 54 bottom, page 62 top, page 64; Tim Street-Porter: page 44; Melinda Sue Gordon: front cover, page 46, page 60, page 91, page 95; Patrick House: page 48 top, page 54 top, page 62 bottom; and Digital Domain: back cover, title page, pages 82–83, pages 86–87, page 89 bottom, page 90, page 92 bottom, page 94 middle and bottom.

Select photographs from the chapter "If the Makeup Was Baked, Did the Caterer Use Rouge for Food Coloring?" by Jurgen Heimann, Kazuhiro Tsuji, and Rick Baker.

contents

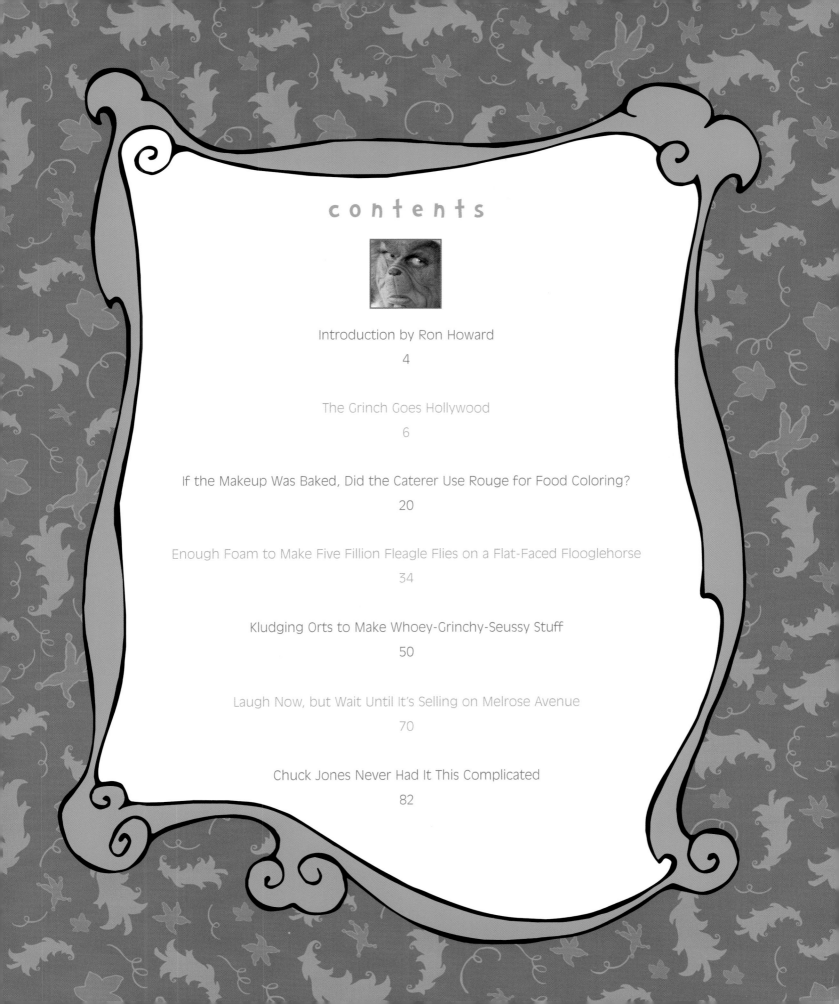

Introduction

As it has done with umpteen zillion "kids of all ages," the story of the Grinch completely enthralled me from my very first encounter.

This amazing Seussian antihero, with his diabolical yuletide heist and irresistibly poignant redemption, never lost any luster for me as the years passed, and I was truly excited when the time came to purchase a new copy of the book so I could share the story with my own kids. They, of course, loved it.

There is no doubt that Dr. Seuss' great grumpy Grinch stands slouched at the very top of my list of all-time favorite characters. He's cool. He's a classic.

So when my partner at Imagine Films, Brian Grazer, excitedly told me he was pursuing the screen rights for a live-action adaptation of the story, you'd think I would've leapt over tables, chairs, or any other obstacles in my way to ensure that I would be the one to take the directorial reins. However, that was not the case. "A great idea for the company," I remember saying, "but probably not for me to direct. Too tough a movie to make," I seem to recall lying. Yes, I was lying. I didn't think the movie would be too challenging. I like challenges. The truth is, I was intimidated by the task. I held the book and character of the Grinch in such high regard that I was unwilling to take responsibility for a live-action film version of the book, which would obviously have to be expanded, and therefore altered, quite a bit.

Brian accepted and supported my position on the subject, but did eventually ask me to help our team at Imagine formulate some basic ideas for the expansion of the story beyond the scope of the original tale. I was happy to pitch in this way, thinking I could still keep my distance, but in fact, as soon as my imagination began embracing the adaptation—well, suffice it to say, the magnetism of that green, hairy, and hilarious Grinch started taking effect. Pile on top of that the news that none other than Jim Carrey wanted to play the Grinch, and my about-face was complete. As a lover of great acting, I found the opportunity to collaborate with Jim on such a funny and unique film character irresistible. I also realized I would kick myself forever for not taking the plunge into the vivid, funny, and weirdly accessible society of Whoville, with its quirks and visual potential.

I was in. As producer, my buddy Brian Grazer had once again excelled in catalyzing a film project with tremendous potential.

Now I was left with that little matter of...well...making the movie. The daunting task of bringing this fantastical world to life would fall not only on my shoulders but also on those of some enormously talented people, whom I was lucky enough to recruit. Their efforts, along with my own, are recounted in this book. While Dr. Seuss created indelible images, he also created memorable words, and our movie is anchored by the work of screenwriters Peter Seaman and Jeffrey Price (with an uncredited but very significant contribution from writers Alec Berg, Jeff Schaffer, and David Mandel), who worked hard and well to expand the book into an inspired motion picture.

In the wake of all the crucial creative decisions that are made, movies also demand that thousands of residual production issues be addressed with foresight, efficiency, imagination, and taste. Much of this responsibility fell to executive producer and second unit director Todd Hallowell, whose passion for problem-solving is prodigious. He positively influenced virtually every phase of the production.

From the earliest production design and storyboard meetings through Rick Baker's painstaking but brilliant evolution of the makeups for the Whos and the Grinch; from the days and nights filming with a wonderful cast and crew through the endless hours in the editing room (with my trusted longtime editors Dan Hanley and Mike Hill); from the earliest preview screenings through the final sound and music mix—I found the filmmaking experience to be thoroughly fascinating and extremely satisfying.

At this writing, I have no idea how our movie will be received by audiences or critics, but I do know this: As lighthearted and unpretentious as *Dr. Seuss' How the Grinch Stole Christmas!* is in tone, I am proud to say that no group of motion picture professionals ever worked harder on a studio movie. The responsibility we all felt to do justice to the great Dr. Seuss and his Christmas antihero, the Grinch, simply demanded that effort.

Ron Howard, Los Angeles, California

The Grinch Goes Hollywood

In February 1999, *How the Grinch Stole Christmas!* was known as the classic 1957 children's book by Dr. Seuss and as the 1966 television program of the same name. As a movie, it existed, as yet, only as a glimmer in the eyes of director Ron Howard and producer Brian Grazer of Imagine Entertainment, who had gone so far as to persuade Jim Carrey to star in it and Universal Pictures to distribute it. But there was no script, no sets, no props, no wardrobe, no makeup design: just Howard with the notion "I think I can make a pretty good movie from this book." One year—a frenetic 365 days later—the sets torn down, the set dressing, props, and costumes all stored, Howard and Grazer walked into screening room 7 at Universal Studios in Hollywood and sat down to watch editors Dan Hanley and Mike Hill's first cut of the movie *Dr. Seuss' How the Grinch Stole Christmas!*

For the first time since he began the movie, Howard was able to come to the studio and not worry about yesterday's, today's, or tomorrow's shooting. He indulged in the luxury of simply enjoying the movie and taking satisfaction

The Grinch begins working on the sleigh in which he will ride down Mt. Crumpit to Whoville to steal Christmas from the Whos. The construction of the sleigh is a montage set to the classic song "You're a Mean One, Mr. Grinch."

7

in the fact that it now actually existed on film. He delighted in Jim Carrey's performance, in the world he and his crew had created, and sat there "rooting for the movie." That afternoon, he would watch it again and begin the process known to directors as "the slaying of the firstborn"—that is, cutting the scenes they *thought* they couldn't live without.

"On nearly every movie, I've had situations that if I was told you cannot shoot that scene, I would have said, 'I quit, I can't do the movie without it,' and in every instance, once I got into the editing room, I cut the scene without a second thought." Editing is a critical juncture in the filmmaking process. Howard must be able to distance himself from the hard work over the past months of filming and be able to look at a shot and say, "Who the heck did *that* shot?" Still, editing is the purest aspect of filmmaking. No politics are

Ron Howard shows Taylor Momsen (Cindy Lou Who) where Mt. Crumpit is in relation to the rest of the Whoville set. Cindy can't understand why everyone is so "kerbobbled" over Christmas, and she questions the very meaning of the holiday. When she discovers that the Grinch hates Christmas, she wants to find out more in the hopes that the Grinch will help her come to terms with her own yuletide doubts.

(top left)
The face behind the slate is Jim Carrey's and, as the Grinch, he's poised atop Mt. Crumpit getting ready to go down to Whoville to steal Christmas. Built of Styrofoam, Mt. Crumpit was shot on Stage 27 at Universal Studios.

(top right)
Jim Carrey and Ron Howard.

(bottom)
Universal Pictures chairman Stacy Snider visits with Jim Carrey on the Whoville set.

A photograph taken by Michael Corenblith in early 1999 of the top of the Solitude Ski Resort near Salt Lake City. The Seussian peaks were added (note the green figure on Mt. Crumpit), as was a rendering of Whoville. This was the basic layout used for reference until Digital Domain began to create the world in greater detail. At the resort, for an entire week In March 2000, a production unit shot the sleigh ride featuring the Grinch, Cindy, and Max.

involved, just hard choices. One director's first cut of a 1999 movie clocked in at a derriere-numbing four hours. The director was pleased with this length and declared to the studio no major cuts needed to be made. The studio, not surprisingly, disagreed.

"Editing is when you can't operate in theories. The time for that is when you're shooting the movie and you have a lot of options as you gather the raw material," notes Howard.

Back in February 1999, Howard knew the visual raw materials—sets, costumes, set dressing, props, and makeup and hair designs—all would have to be fabricated from scratch. *Dr. Seuss' How the Grinch Stole Christmas!* turned out to be a movie that was so large in scope—and replete with complicated technical issues, all of which did not come cheap (less expensive than *Titanic*; more than *The Blair Witch Project*)—that nothing could be taken for granted. "It took what should have been the sheer, giddy pleasure out of it for me, but every now and then I could relax and be amazed that I was actually standing in the middle of Whoville," says Howard. It was all inspired by Dr. Seuss' brilliant character the Grinch, who, as Seuss' biographers Judith and Neil Morgan wrote, "had become as vivid a character to Americans as Charles Dickens' Scrooge."

While he was expending time and energy on the movie's visuals, Howard was equally preoccupied with the other half of the raw material: the script, and how to keep developing the characters in a way that he understood and related to while acknowledging the whimsy and imagination of Dr. Seuss' fable. "To be honest, I really don't think in vivid, visual terms," says Howard. "I think in psychological and emotional conditions, and then the visual world is something I can come to understand. All movies—even fantasy—begin with character for me."

1 3

(top)
The Brothers Grinch. Goaded by Jim Carrey to experience the discomfort first-hand, Ron Howard (right) dressed up as the Grinch for one day. Howard arrived at 4:30 A.M. to go through the makeup and was amused during the morning, a little annoyed by lunch, and by the end of the day...thoroughly uncomfortable.

(bottom)
Producer Brian Grazer and his Imagine Entertainment partner, Ron Howard. Since its inception in 1986, Imagine has produced thirty-six movies with a total worldwide gross of $3.5 billion. *Dr. Seuss' How the Grinch Stole Christmas!* is number thirty-seven.

The fantasy genre was certainly not new territory for Howard. **Splash** and **Cocoon** touched upon that world while **Willow** was fully immersed in it. "Since I come at things from a logical and rational place, I always love when fantasies logically add up for me. If I can get emotionally involved, then I have a foothold to get into the story." Howard nearly echoes what Dr. Seuss—whose real name was Theodor Geisel—said in 1949: "Children analyze fantasy. They know you're kidding them. There's got to be logic in the way you kid them. Their fun is pretending...making believe they believe it."

As opposed to his partner, Grazer does think in vivid, visual terms. A painter by avocation, he has very strong opinions about how color works in an overall mosaic. "I wanted the movie to be visually stimulating in an original way," says Grazer. "The design is exciting and the color works with it to make something I really haven't seen before. I wanted the visual team to create an original and complex world, but one which also has a level of irreverence and sophistication that would be cool for kids."

Nearly all of the forty-four books written and illustrated by Dr. Seuss were constructed as fables that touch on issues in modern society, featuring characters grappling with eternal issues of love, strength, weakness, desire, fear, loyalty. Geisel believed that, except for their vivid imagery, classical myths were lost on children, and so his themes were cloaked in his wondrous, zany, archetypal visual style. For adults and children alike, this style gave a lasting and vivid resonance to his entertaining stories.

How did Howard and Grazer get the rights to do the story in the first place? None of Dr. Seuss' books has ever been developed as a live-action motion picture. Audrey Geisel, the widow of Theodor (Ted) Geisel, had resisted previous overtures from Hollywood precisely because she believed her husband had an ambivalent feeling toward the movie business: "Ted was too avant-garde for Hollywood." **The 5,000 Fingers of Dr. T.**, the 1953 film Geisel wrote, was not a pleasant experience for him and was his first and last encounter with live-action features. "The animated version of **The Grinch** [written by Geisel and directed by Chuck Jones in 1966] was a classic that Ted was extremely happy with, so he felt, why challenge it?" Mrs. Geisel adds.

Earthquake…Educational… Eggs…Electric…here it is, Electrolysis! High up in his lair on Mt. Crumpit, the Grinch flips through the Whoville phone book, reveling in his loathing for the residents.

"But with the technological advances in the last few years, which would allow Ted's world to be faithfully re-created, I just felt like the time was right," says Mrs. Geisel. It was then that her representatives sent word to the Hollywood community that offers to make the book into a movie would be entertained.

"I went to her home in La Jolla (California) and pitched her our story idea, and I could tell she was going south on it, and I said, 'I can tell this isn't working for you,' and she said, 'It just doesn't seem right,'" recalls Grazer. "I pleaded with her for one more chance before she made her decision, but she was sort of noncommittal.

"I spent the next week with Ron retooling the story and I kept begging her to let me have one more day in court with her, and she finally agreed to the second meeting and it was enough for her to wipe all the other proposals off the table.

"Audrey is very passionate about protecting the spirit and integrity of her husband's work, but at the same time she wanted to be smart and business-like about it."

After being selected by Dr. Seuss Enterprises, the Imagine partners had to get their star. Recalls Howard: "I called Jim Carrey and told him, 'I want to make this movie, and all I can tell you about it is what is in the book. I'm asking you to take a leap of faith,' and, God bless him, he did."

"I always saw Jim as the Grinch," notes Grazer. "Jim is always at his best as an actor when he is proactive, when he animates and when power is central to his character. So the intersection of what the Grinch is all about thematically and what Jim Carrey is about as a performer, is a perfect combination."

Audrey Geisel still wanted to be sure that Carrey would be the perfect Grinch, so she met with him while he was filming *Man on the Moon*, when

(top left)
Director of photography Don Peterman—who has shot *Splash*, *Cocoon*, and *Gung Ho* for Howard—was nominated for an Academy Award for *Flashdance* and *Star Trek IV: The Voyage Home*.

(top right)
I can tell by that Santa hat you're not a real doctor. Jeffrey Tambor, who plays Mayor May Who, enjoys a moment between takes with Jim Carrey and second unit director (and executive producer) Todd Hallowell. Interesting side note: When Carrey first came to Los Angeles, Tambor was a substitute instructor at Carrey's acting class.

(middle)
The crew meets one week before shooting to read through the script and address any final problems or questions individual departments might have regarding filming. At the head of the table is Ron Howard; to his right is first assistant director Aldric Porter, who runs the meeting; to Howard's left is executive producer Todd Hallowell and to his left, unit production manager David Womark.

(bottom)
Ron Howard rehearses the Whoville residents in the scene in which Cindy nominates the Grinch to be Wholiday Cheermeister.

18

Carrey was totally immersed in the role of the late comedian Andy Kaufman. "She came to my trailer and Andy did his impression of me doing the Grinch," recalls Carrey with a laugh. "It got a little complex, but it was there for her."

"I was stunned. Without any makeup, he simply became the Grinch before my eyes," recalls Mrs. Geisel, who thinks her husband would have approved. "Ted would have totally embraced Jim Carrey as the Grinch. Actually, they [Ted and Jim] are alike in many ways and are two very, very unique individuals," says Mrs. Geisel.

"I was flabbergasted when Audrey signed off on the deal because the Grinch was such an indelible part of my childhood," says Carrey. "It simply wasn't Christmas without our family reading the book and watching the cartoon."

"It's a real world, it's just not our world," was the guiding principle Howard exhorted his creative team to follow as they began work on creating Whoville. Every element of the movie had to be built from scratch, and every actor had to go through an extensive makeup and hair application to truly embody the art of Dr. Seuss. Extensive and innovative visual effects were called for. Nonetheless, these stylistic issues still had to take a back seat to Howard's desire to tell a genuine story with emotional resonance.

Every story and style choice became its own house of cards, and while not always precarious, the film became a complicated and often byzantine construct compounded of daunting logistics, inspired craftsmanship, and, hopefully, art.

If the Makeup Was Baked, Did the Caterer Use Rouge for Food Coloring?

In December 1998, Rick Baker had his design for the Grinch makeup applied to his own face in a three-hour procedure. A month earlier, Ron Howard had let Baker know that he was interested in seeing what the Grinch could look like, to be sure making *Dr. Seuss' How the Grinch Stole Christmas!* was even viable.

Despite having worked on dozens of films over twenty-five years, Baker was looking at the greatest challenge of his career. He would have to create the Grinch's makeup, the Grinch's green-hair suit, and 125 other makeups for the Whos of Whoville. As Baker examined his finished makeup design in the mirror, he was "pretty happy." Aside from his salt-and-pepper ponytail, Baker looked just like he had always imagined the Grinch.

Baker knew that if the picture did become a go, his

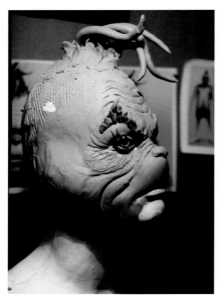

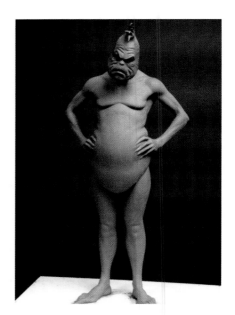

Details of an early Grinch maquette by Rick Baker.

makeup for the Grinch was on the mark, although it would take another seven months to get everyone to agree with him. Intensely focused while working, and very funny when not, Baker is entirely unfettered by the politics of Hollywood and tends to say whatever is on his mind (a not surprising result of winning five Academy Awards).

"Re-creating what Dr. Seuss drew [would not be] a workable makeup, what with the Grinch's oversized almond-shaped eyes, huge muzzle, and long neck," says Baker. The initial design he tried on himself was a bit worrisome to Ron Howard and Brian Grazer. "At first, they were afraid that he was too covered up and no one would know it was Jim Carrey under there. Jim, himself, thought it was too constraining and that he wouldn't be able to move his face around," says Baker. "The makeup was never going to be as if Jim had nothing on his face."

Says Grazer: "I wanted Jim Carrey to have the most amount of leeway in the makeup to anthropomorphize. The Grinch is about power, so I wanted Rick to create something that gave Jim the freedom to make the character powerful."

In March 1999, Baker and his team made a full-body plaster cast of Jim Carrey before he left to shoot on location for the movie *Me, Myself & Irene.*

Because of these various concerns, Baker began designing other Grinch makeups, with Carrey periodically coming to Baker's Cinovation Studio to try them out. One day in July 1999, after going though a dozen Grinch makeups, Carrey saw the photo of Baker in the Grinch makeup from December 1998. "This is it. This is what the Grinch should be," said Carrey. Coming full circle, the Imagine partners realized that no one can do what Jim Carrey can. Despite having his entire face covered (including yellow-tinted contact lenses in his eyes), it was apparent after the first film test that anything less than a full-on makeup was, as Howard termed it, "a Hollywood cheat." "The most important aspect of the makeup was that I really wanted to make it look authentic and in the spirit of Seuss," says Carrey. "We even tried painting my face, which would have been very comfortable and given me a lot of leeway, but I looked like someone from the cast of *Cats.*"

An early life cast Baker made of the Grinch in an attempt to determine the shape of the body.

"You could actually take Jim and seven other people, put them in the Grinch makeup, have them stand in a lineup, and it would be impossible to pick out Jim. But the minute they start moving and talking, there's no question. On film, he totally embodies the character," adds Howard.

All the actors in the movie donned fake teeth Cinovation sculpted from dental acrylic. The Grinch's teeth, however, were much more complex (almost like a full denture) and forced Carrey to "get around" the teeth, and thus the letter "s" came out sounding akin to a Sean Connery–like "sh."

"I was always confident in that makeup because the movie is called

Dr. Seuss' How the Grinch Stole Christmas!, not *How Jim Carrey Stole Christmas!* It was important that he was the Grinch playing the Grinch, not Jim Carrey playing the Grinch," says Baker.

All the actors in the movie donned fake teeth sculpted by Cinovation from dental acrylic. The Grinch's teeth, however, were much more complex (almost like a full set of dentures).

Josh Ryan Evans (bottom row, two left photos), as the young Grinch, is shown trying on teeth made from dental acrylic and after his first makeup test. Other shots show Baker's early attempts at what the Whos should look like.

Finally, in February 2000, after having been made up by makeup artist Kazuhiro Tsuji eighty times, Jim Carrey wrapped on the movie, and after thanking the crew for its hard work and patience, he added this tongue-in-cheek coda: "To my makeup crew, I want to give a special thank-you and I never want to see you again!"

There was no getting around the fact that the makeup (three rubber facial pieces which were baked at 250 degrees for six hours) was a huge hindrance for Carrey, taking three hours to put on and thirty minutes to remove. Despite the inconvenience, the makeup was thin enough for Carrey to move his face to express any kind of nuance. In his one-of-a-kind hand-sewn, dyed-yak-hair Grinch outfit, also created by Baker, Carrey would work up quite a sweat, and he also had to deal with his Grinch teeth occasionally coming loose when he talked, not to mention the continual irritation of his yellow-tinted contact lenses (which covered the entire eyeball).

Makeup artist Kazuhiro Tsuji puts the finishing touches on Jim Carrey. Carrey's face consisted of three rubber foam pieces that had to be baked for six hours at 250 degrees, and the success rate of usable pieces was around fifty percent. For all the actors in the movie, Cinovation had to come up with over eight thousand facial pieces—which means they made close to double that amount.

With the combination of make-up, lenses, teeth, and suit, it was "like being buried alive in the ground by kidnappers and all you get is a straw so you can breathe—on a daily basis," recalls Carrey. The first few weeks of shooting in September and early October were quite a psychological challenge for Carrey. "I was late a lot because I had to psych myself up to the fact that once I left my house, the next stop was the makeup trailer. I finally realized how adaptable humans are, because it's truly not possible to live in the whole getup, but I learned to live with it because I didn't want to be miserable the entire shoot. Funny thing was, the minute Ron said 'Action,' I totally lost the sensation of discomfort."

Carrey was successful in persuading Howard to wear the Grinch makeup and suit for an entire day so that he could really experience what the process entailed. Howard arrived at 4:30 A.M. and he recalls the first couple hours as fun, "but then I really got uncomfortable."

(top left)
As a member of the Whoville band, Verne Troyer (who played Mini Me in *Austin Powers: The Spy Who Shagged Me*) gets touched up by Rick Baker.

(top right)
Of course, I can still karaoke, I didn't put in the fake teeth. After being encouraged by Jim Carrey to put on the Grinch makeup and costume for a day, Ron Howard deftly uses headphones to keep his hat in place.

(bottom left)
Ron Howard and Jim Carrey.

Richard Snell puts the finishing touches on Heather Gerdes.

"Ron never did the (contact) lenses, though," adds Carrey. "That's the thing that pushes you over Niagara. Add a little synthetic snow in the eyes and you'll be blubbering at the end of the day."

Baker got into the spirit of things by getting into Who makeup as an extra for the Whobilation sequence.

As sure as Baker had been about his first Grinch design, he was totally per-plexed as to what the Whos should look like. "The hardest aspect of the movie was figuring out what the Whos were supposed to look like," says Baker. "Even Audrey Geisel was not exactly sure. She told me she always thought the Whos were sort of like insects." Initially, Baker and his staff did literal translations from the book. The results were a little too scary, as far as Howard and Grazer

this page:
(top left)
The Timekeeper, played by Rance Howard, Ron Howard's father.

(top right)
Cindy Lou Who, played by Taylor Momsen.

(bottom right)
Bill Irwin—who plays Lou Lou Who, the befuddled postmaster of Whoville—and Taylor Momsen.

facing page:
(top left)
Molly Shannon during her makeup test with makeup artist Kenny Myers. All cast members—even featured extras—had to come to Rick Baker's Glendale studio for makeup tests.

(top right)
Rick Baker makes up his daughter, Rebecca, as a Who child.

(bottom)
Stage 16 was converted into the hair and makeup staging area. During the busiest days on the Whoville set, more than sixty makeup artists and twenty hairstylists began their day as early as 2:30 A.M. for a 7:00 A.M. shooting call. The process for the ninety actors (including wardrobe) took between three and four hours.

were concerned. The Imagine partners wanted to make sure the Whos were more human-looking so that the audience would relate to them. A turning point came for Baker when he watched the 1966 Chuck Jones cartoon and realized that the animated Cindy was actually more human-looking than the Whos in the book. He and his crew set off in the direction of balancing the Seuss-like look with the desire of the filmmakers to make the Whos appealingly human. This was partially accomplished when Baker made the decision to put full wigs on the Whos, which, in turn, necessitated bringing in a number of hairstylists. In order to pull this off, he brought Gail Ryan on board to help create the hairstyles.

Beginning in July at Baker's studio, Ryan and her crew eventually came up with two hundred hair designs. "What

The stage floor at Rick Baker's Cinovation Studio, where around 1,200 production molds of all the Whos (and the Grinch) were assembled after filming wrapped and before they were sent to storage.

I always wanted out of any design was a sense of whimsy," notes Ryan. "Sometimes I wanted the hair suspended in the air, defying gravity, much like the Whos do in the movie," she adds.

From a practical point of view, Baker was always worried about the Who children. With the labor laws that limit the number of hours young people may work, production could not afford to have kids in a two-hour makeup process. Thus, the theory was cooked up that the older a Who gets, the more "Whoey" or "Seussian" his or her features become. Witness the difference between Cindy and the timekeeper, played by Rance Howard.

After the artistic questions had been settled, staggering logistics had to be dealt with. How to get 110 actors through makeup, hair, and wardrobe for the thirty-five days of filming in Whoville?

Baker and his foreman, Bill Sturgeon, assembled a team of sixty makeup artists and twenty hairstylists, which operated out of Universal's Stage 16

The Grinch and Sherman Klump (played by Eddie Murphy) with the man who created both makeup designs: Rick Baker. For a time, *Dr. Seuss' How the Grinch Stole Christmas!* and *Nutty Professor II: The Klumps* were shooting side by side on the Universal lot.

along with the costume department. "The scale of the movie was something I always was hoping would come along in my career. I grew up with *The Wizard of Oz* and the original *Planet of the Apes*, both movies that inspired me to do what I do," says Baker. In fact, the hair and makeup in those movies are dwarfed by *Dr. Seuss' How the Grinch Stole Christmas!*, since in *The Wizard of Oz*, the Munchkins wore bald caps and fancy wigs, and in *Planet of the Apes*, the biggest makeup days involved, at most, twenty actors.

Baker's staff at Cinovation Studios was responsible for making the rubber facial pieces for each actor. Each facial piece could be used only once. Jim Carrey worked eighty days on the movie, which meant that with his three-piece masks, 240 pieces had to be made, each of which took 7½ hours to bake at 145 degrees. All told, more than 8,000 facial pieces, 3,500 ears, 300 wigs, and 150 facial-hair pieces were made, all of which necessitated Cinovation's running crews day and night to get ready for filming. And, as if that were not already enough, Baker and company were simultaneously at work on the Imagine Entertainment movie *Nutty Professor II: The Klumps*, the follow-up

this page:
The Whoman genome project. Josh Ryan Evans, who plays the young Grinch, with the animatronic puppet created by Baker's Cinovation Studios.

facing page:
Rick Baker and his team at Cinovation designed the animatronic Grinch puppet that was operated by radio control. This puppet could articulate nearly every possible facial feature. Rick Baker (seated on left) controlled the eyes; Mark Setrakian (seated on right) controlled all the other facial features. The gross body movements—neck, arms, legs—were controlled through rods by Jurgen Heimann (above Setrakian) and Tim Blainey (above Heimann). Also pictured are Aaron Sims (with slate) and Bill Sturgeon, Cinovation shop foreman. Another puppet was made for the scene of the infant Grinch floating to Whoville in a pumbrasella, which was entirely radio-controlled.

to the 1996 box-office smash *The Nutty Professor.* Somewhat easing the workload was that, most of the time, both films were shot on the Universal Studios lot.

All the actors and extras in *The Grinch* were designated as one of three makeup categories. A Number 1 actor was someone with dialogue or involved in a close-up and went through a three-hour process with full makeup. Number 2 was a featured extra, and her makeup took ninety minutes and consisted of a muzzle piece that raised the nose and lengthened the upper lip. A Number 3 was an extra used only as background and limited to face coloring and a fancy hairstyle. Broken down by category, Cinovation created makeups for sixty-eight Number 1's, fifty-six Number 2's, forty-five Number 3's, and thirty-four child-character makeups.

Enough Foam to Make Five Fillion Fleagle Flies on a Flat-Faced Flooglehorse

"**H**e's not the guy with the cape and beret" is how set decorator Merideth Boswell once described production designer Michael Corenblith. In Hollywood, cutting-edge sensibilities often are announced with a distinctive flair in clothing, body art, and/or pierced body parts. For example, one cameraman changed his very common name to a very uncommon name, shaved his head, pierced both ears, wore only snowboard/surf wear (he does neither sport), purchased a vintage four-wheel-drive vehicle, and became *the* guy. Corenblith's standard outfit of button-down shirt, blue jeans, and tennis shoes might be more in keeping with the image of an architecture professor at UCLA. Then again, with an Academy Award nomination for *Apollo 13* and a couple dozen design credits, he doesn't need an act.

One of the questions the filmmakers were asked most during the creation of the movie was "How are you going to make a movie from that little book?" As in many of Dr. Seuss' books, a moral lesson was the fulcrum of the story, but from a visual standpoint, that lesson per se didn't offer Corenblith a lot of clues.

The drawing technique Seuss employed for *The Grinch* was relatively simple. Early on, the filmmakers considered making the sets appear as if drawn and thus remaining rigorously faithful to the book. But that idea, while appealing to Dr. Seuss purists, would leave the movie "looking amateurish, like regional theater," according to executive producer and second unit director Todd Hallowell.

Corenblith wanted to keep the visual style within the limits of what Dr. Seuss had done, even though the script greatly expanded upon the original story, so he proposed to Ron Howard that the movie be a celebration of the visual style Geisel created, or an amalgam of the art in all of his books. In their initial meeting, Howard, Hallowell, and Corenblith looked at three distinct Seuss books: *The 500 Hats of Bartholomew Cubbins* (1937), *Horton Hears a Who!* (the first appearance of Whos, in 1954), and *Oh, the Places You'll Go!* (1990).

"What I wanted to do was pull something from the beginning, middle, and end of Seuss' career," says Corenblith. This study revealed that Geisel, over the

course of his career, worked with a vocabulary of style, forms, and shapes that was, in turn, derived or abstracted from true architectural styles. Geisel had an obvious love of the work of the ingenious Spanish architect Antoni Gaudí, and also was enamored of Moroccan and Islamic architecture. "Through all of the books, one can see a set of shapes that he was attracted to and that would appear throughout his career, so we knew there was something very archetypal and true and good about those things," says Corenblith.

Thus, the set for Whoville turned out to be a Who version of a World's Fair. The town hall is Greek Revival, with the Seuss animals guarding the entrance reminiscent of the lions on the steps of the New York Public Library. Farfingles Department Store features the Art Nouveau shapes of an old Parisian storefront; the old biddies live in a New

© Ramon Manent/CORBIS

3 7

Whobilation 1000 is in full swing, presided over by Mayor May Who (Jeffrey Tambor) and his sycophantic assistant, Who Bris (Clint Howard), on the steps of Whoville's city hall. Note the Seussian animals on each end of the Whoville city hall, inspired by the New York Public Library (see inset below). Behind the building is a thirty-foot-tall blue screen that surrounded the stage and would later be replaced with digitally created buildings and sky by the visual effects company Digital Domain.

© Gail Mooney/CORBIS

(right)
Who houses under construction on the Universal back lot. In the background is a Styrofoam berm created to block a set from *Jurassic Park*. After production, the houses were moved one hundred yards and now sit next door to the Bates Motel on the back lot.

(below)
Two of the clay maquettes designed in spring 1999 by production designer Michael Corenblith represent his first concepts of Whoville. At top is Whoville city hall and at bottom is part of the town square, which includes the post office and hat store. Both maquettes quite closely resemble what was finally constructed.

Orleans French Quarter–style apartment; the grocery store has an Islamic feel to it. And the post office? Pure Gaudí.

"When Michael showed me photographs of Gaudí's buildings and then his clay model of Whoville, I knew the concept was going to fly," says Howard.

But before the buildings could be finalized, art had to take a back seat to the realities (financial, logistical, engineering) of creating such a world, primarily because in one world of Dr. Seuss', no straight lines exist.

Corenblith's essentially Seussian structures had to support weight and connect one space to another. Construction coordinator Terry Scott found a structural engineer, Michael Johnson, who worked for Jet Propulsion Laboratory in Pasadena and who also engineered floats for the Rose Parade. Using state-of-the-art techniques, Johnson validated that the structures Corenblith wanted to build were structurally viable.

The best way to capture these wild architectural forms was to sculpt them first as clay models and then carve the sets out of Styrofoam—and so much of it that if the Styrofoam used for all the sets were cut into standard lumber dimensions and laid end to end, it would run for nearly six hundred miles.

The Whoville set was built over the course of eighteen weeks on Stage 12—at thirty thousand square feet and with fifty-foot ceilings, the largest on the Universal lot. Every bit of space was used. The buildings were constructed out of Styrofoam over a steel armature, which was then covered with eight different applications of plaster. Each structure stood apart from the others.

If all the Styrofoam used in building the sets were cut into standard board length and laid end to end, it would run for nearly six hundred miles. The construction of the cave (above) was achieved by sculpting from rectangular blocks.

Through his use of diagonals, bridges, stairs, spirals, and archways that defied gravity, Geisel's books conveyed enormous dynamism. Geisel's work was one-dimensional, and he never had to worry about trivial matters like the laws of physics. But Corenblith did.

"I really wanted to take all color out of the Grinch's world and make it cold, like a black-and-white movie," notes Corenblith. "And this did create problems in terms of lighting."

"Oh, yeah," recalls Peterman. "The cave was a bit tricky. When I first saw the plans, I thought we were dead, because it was so high I didn't know what to do. Then they put holes in the ceiling so that we could put twelve xenons [lights] that would represent daylight or moonlight coming through the cracks of the cave." Peterman could then hide mirrors on the ground to bounce the light from the xenons back into other areas of the dark cave walls in order to bring out some detail.

No right angles or straight lines were employed anywhere except on the interior of the post office, and the illusion of curved walls was painstakingly created. The wallpaper and the angle at which the walls were joined were used in tandem to create the appearance of a curved wall.

With this no right angles rule, the building of the various structures was a tricky business, no better illustrated than with the construction of Farfingles

facing page:
With its spiral ramp, the Grinch's cave was inspired by the Guggenheim Museum in New York City. Corenblith used it to great advantage in the scene in which Cindy invites the Grinch to the Whobilation. The scene starts on the floor (next to the giant monkey) and ends at the top of the ramp (above the monkey).

this page:
(left)
Ron Howard and crew on Mt. Crumpit.

(right)
Ron Howard rehearses Taylor Momsen and Jim Carrey. This is the scene in which Cindy Lou has come to the Grinch's cave to invite him to be Wholiday Cheermeister for Whoville's Whobilation. Standing behind them is Taylor's dialogue coach, Marnie Cooper.

For construction coordinator Terry Scott, the single most difficult structure was the Farfingles Department Store. Plexiglas windows, which were needed so that the camera could shoot from inside to out and outside in, were difficult to seat into the sparse exterior supports. The fact that the bottom of the structure was smaller than the middle only exacerbated the situation.

Department Store. For that structure, Scott was faced with the difficult task of building both the interior and exterior of a sphere, with one entire side of the sphere open so that the camera could shoot from the inside to the out-side. The seemingly simple task of trying to make a door open and close became infinitely more complicated when a door had to operate in a com-pound curve.

The layout of the village of Whoville arose out of what Corenblith deduced was Geisel's love of medieval architecture (as evidenced in *The King's Stilts*, *The 500 Hats of Bartholomew Cubbins*, and *Bartholomew and the Oobleck*), even though in *How the Grinch Stole Christmas!*, Geisel depicted

Whoville merely as a series of haystack houses. The Christmas tree is anchored in the middle of the village square, with the buildings radiating outward from it like spokes. Viewed from above, the bricks on the plaza spiral away from the hub of the tree, with the village as center of the universe. The buildings were designed to convey a sense of the history of Whoville, in the same way that villages in Europe reflect centuries of habitation. "What I was trying not to do," says Corenblith, "was build something that looked like a Santa's Village that was dropped into place." Hence, the variety of styles in Whoville are supposed to reflect changing tastes over many years.

Corenblith and art director Dan Webster pored over all the Dr. Seuss books and developed a palette that included the major parts of the color wheel, but was still keyed to the colors Geisel used in his books. Since very little in the movie is taken directly from the book, attention to form and the polychromatic—without being too bright—result in a new yet somehow authentic Seussian world.

The hugeness of the set and other considerations made director of photography Don Peterman's job a bit problematic. With Jim Carrey on screen for

Production designer Michael
Corenblith in Whoville.

4 5

A sequence cut from the movie was a lighting contest between neighbors Martha May Whovier (Christine Baranski, on the roof of the house on the left) and Betty Lou Who (Molly Shannon, on the roof of the house on the right). This scene "was really hard to cut because it's funny and visually exciting," notes Ron Howard. "Every director has the same story of the great scene they had to leave on the floor."

most of the movie, Peterman had to shoot the scenes without Carrey during the three hours he spent in makeup every morning. Because the floor of the set was decorative, moving heavy lighting equipment across the set was not an option, so Peterman and gaffer Gary Palmer devised a system whereby nearly all the lights on 2,200 channels were controlled by a single dimmer board. In addition, the 52,000 Christmas lights that decorated all the Whoville buildings actually lit the buildings perfectly. "If I had had to light the buildings in a conventional sense, we would still be shooting," said Peterman some months after the movie wrapped. "It took a couple months to figure out the set lighting design, but once we figured it out, it was easy to shoot on that

set." For the most part, the only lights on the floor were a Chinese lantern, fluorescent lights on sticks, and a flashlight used to illuminate actors' eyes in close-ups.

Corenblith envisioned the Grinch's cave as a space reflecting the Grinch's nature: not angry, but hurt. The architecture of the cave helped support this interpretation of the character. One of the images Corenblith impressed upon Howard when he described the cave to him was Charles Foster Kane walking alone through the giant rooms of Xanadu in *Citizen Kane*.

The closest source material for the cave was probably Carlsbad Caverns, in New Mexico, although the geometric stalactites and stalagmites imbued the set with an even more cathedral-like atmosphere. The other architectural aspect that really tied in to the Grinch's kinetic character (and, more to the point, Jim Carrey's) was the spiral ramp, reminiscent of that in Frank Lloyd

As originally designed, the Grinch's cave was entirely enclosed, which director of photography Don Peterman realized would ultimately hinder shooting. To properly light the walls and spaces in and around the stalactites and stalagmites, Peterman needed ambient light from a hidden source. Holes were cut into the ceiling of the cave to simulate daylight or moonlight leaking through cracks in the stone. Peterman then hid mirrors on the floor of the cave to reflect light into the darker recesses. "The scenes in the cave are my favorites," says Ron Howard. "The set really embodies the Grinch's neuroses." The set (below right) was inspired by natural caves such as those in Carlsbad, New Mexico (below left).

facing page:
(top)
Martha May Whovier's kitchen. The elegance of her character is reflected structurally in the higher ceilings and more graceful curves in contrast to the Lou house (bottom). Lower ceilings and homier furnishings reflect a workingman's taste.

this page:
(top)
The paper snow used to adorn the Mt. Crumpit set was stirred up by fans and the air-conditioning system. Jim Carrey was entirely encased in his yak-hair Grinch suit and rubber makeup facial appliances. The sets were cooled to between 55 and 58 degrees so that his makeup would remain intact.

(bottom)
The Whoville set.

Wright's Guggenheim Museum in New York City, which permitted Carrey a lot of freedom and spontaneity. To that point, the scene in which Cindy invites the Grinch to the Whobilation utilizes nearly the entire set.

Construction on the interiors was started in the summer of 1999 and extended through to the winter. Over the months, the building process was continuously refined and updated. By the end of the shoot, the crew's building technique had changed radically.

Kludging Orts to Make Whoey-Grinchy-Seussy Stuff

They spawned some unusually contorted conjugated adjectives (Seussy, Seussian) and provided numerous requests along the lines of "Can I have it after the movie is done?" or "Are there any extras?" They usually refer to wardrobe, props, or set decoration—and there *is* a difference between the last two. A prop is an item the actor handles (cigarettes and lighter) and set decoration is not handled (the ashtray)—most of the time. If an actor is having breakfast at the dining room table, the dishes are set decoration and the food and drink are props. If, however, the actor eats in bed, then everything becomes a prop since it's not a typical setting for a meal. Can you figure out who does what in the following scene?

Following a successful day of Grinching in Whoville, the Grinch returns to his cave with his canine companion, Max. He throws

facing page:
Did anyone ever tell you that you look like Rosie the maid from The Jetsons? The Grinch's periscope, designed by Michael Corenblith and built by Allen Hall's special effects shop, through which the Grinch is about to survey the devastation he has wrought down below in Whoville.

this page:
Mayor May Who's bedside table and the coveted Wholiday Cheermeister Award from the Whobilation. The award was the Grinch's, until he more or less rejected his title by burning down the Christmas tree.

this page:
After being humiliated by Mayor May Who, the Grinch gives the Whos a taste of his own version of Christmas cheer and then flees Whoville in a tiny Who car.

facing page:
(top)
The dictum of "no straight lines in Whoville" extended even to the smallest of props.

(bottom left)
Set dressing from Mayor May Who's bedroom. A potter by avocation, set decorator Merideth Boswell experimented with various designs of cups and saucers before settling on this style. The flea-market lamp and the old dial telephone were Seussified in the on-site prop shop.

(bottom right)
Cindy Lou's phonograph, on which she plays her song lamenting the spiritual loss of Christmas. Property master Emily Ferry fashioned it from a 1945 General Electric model. The spinning ballerina was a touch added by prop shop foreman Jim Roberts.

a bag of toxic waste (1) at a poster (2) of the mayor, then takes the elevator lift (3) to change his clothes (4). The Grinch checks out his heart on an X-ray machine (5), then jumps on his bed (6) and listens to his answering machine (7); next he takes a cable (8) that drops him in a recliner (9), and chews on a glass bottle (10).

Answers: 1, props; 2, set decoration; 3, special effects; 4, wardrobe; 5, props; 6, set decoration; 7, props; 8, special effects; 9, set decoration; 10, props. Don't feel bad; a surprising number of professional film reviewers simply refer to it all as props and a lot of film crew personnel don't know the difference.

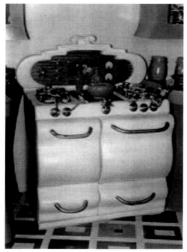

When Ron Howard saw the Seussified Mixmaster blender, he knew the movie was headed stylistically in the right direction. The prop shop coined the style Blizzard Deco to describe this item and others. "It sort of looked like it was caught in a snowdrift," notes property master Emily Ferry.

(bottom)
A 1950s era Wedgewood stove. Good friend George Lucas suggested to Howard that he alter 1950s appliances because of their time-tested design.

In general, a property master and set decorator work closely, but probably never as closely on a movie as Merideth Boswell, the decorator, and Emily Ferry, the prop master, did on *Dr. Seuss' How the Grinch Stole Christmas!* An immeasurable asset was that every single set decoration and prop was built on the Universal lot in a prop shop created specifically for the production. It enabled each department to see immediately what the other was doing so there was no chance of a stylistic collision of a prop and set decoration. "I've never before worked with a prop master whom I shared not only an art background with, but also a similar vision of how things need to look," says Boswell.

But the first order of business in the spring of 1999 was to figure out what was Seuss and what was not, and no one ever came up with a definition except for "I know it when I see it." Furniture, mailboxes, bicycles, cars, most kitchen appliances, telephones, signs—just about every detailed item in the movie—do not have visual references in the book. And ones that actually do were sometimes problematic. "The roast beast as depicted in the book when the Grinch takes it from the refrigerator looks disturbingly like a poodle," notes Ferry. "It was not right for our purpose, but then you think, How dare I depart from the concept of the roast beast? What right do we have to tamper with Dr. Seuss' work?" The one section of the book that was nearly a literal translation was the scene of the feast on the S-shaped table that plays as the movie's finale.

As production designer, Michael Corenblith was the overlord when difficult decisions came up. He had to create a visual world that was consistent among all the departments and that held its logic within the parameters of the script. For example, in the scene when Cindy Lou Who enters a house, sits on a couch, and turns on her blabacorder to interview the two old biddies, that

While the book inspired the movie, this was one scene that was almost a literal translation from the book. The finale, with all the Whos gathering around the S-shaped table and the Grinch carving the roast beast, probably would have been set down in Whoville had the script strictly adhered to the book. As it happened, Howard decided that it would be more emotionally satisfying if the Whos were to come up to the Grinch's home.

house, the couch, Cindy's outfit, the blabacorder, and the biddies cannot all be the same color or in any way detract from whatever the director wants to accomplish in that scene.

"Early on, we decided that we would make this movie as if it were the year Dr. Seuss wrote the book, which is 1957," said executive producer Todd Hallowell. "We strenuously tried to not use materials [invented] after that year."

The preternaturally optimistic Whos reflect the spirit of the United States from the 1933 election of Franklin D. Roosevelt through the euphoria of the post–World War II years, a period during which Dr. Seuss created some of his most enduring works.

"The optimism was reflected in his designs, because Americans in those days believed anything was possible, and they were out to prove it," says

Hallowell. "Art Deco, Streamline, Moderne were of that time and gave a definite feeling of optimism. It all felt like rocket ships."

Fortunately for the creative team, Geisel made Whoville closer to our world than the environments in any other of his books, while still adhering to the signature Seuss shapes and forms. This is most obviously reflected in the book when the Grinch opens the refrigerator, emblazoned with the script "General Wholectric," and removes the roast beast.

In the spring of 1999, Ron Howard had talked to George Lucas about the movie and the daunting task of building a world from scratch. "George told me that when he made *Star Wars* he used European antiques and tweaked them to fit his set deco-ration. His theory was that these items are foreign enough to our culture that we might not know exactly what they were, but [we would recognize that] they did have functions," says Howard. "Merideth had been thinking along the same lines, and, oddly enough, she talked to me about the same thing a few hours later that day."

The direct results of this thinking can be seen in the stoves in the Lou Who house and in Martha May Whovier's house. Both are early 1950s Wedgewood stoves accented with the appropriate Seussian flourishes. "I thought older stoves with the larger knobs and rounded corners had a scale to them that was sort of funny and happy," says Boswell.

Everyone agreed they did not want the props and set decorations to have a cartoon-like quality, bulky and obviously made of foam. What worked so well for the *Flintstones* movies would not work for this film. "Dr. Seuss had an ele-

facing page:
Outraged that the Whos should invite him to their Whobilation on such short notice, the Grinch checks to see whether he can squeeze it into his busy schedule.

"Four o'clock: Wallow in self-pity."

"Four-thirty: Stare into the abyss."

"Five o'clock: Solve world hunger...tell no one."

"Five-thirty: Jazzercise."

"Six-thirty: Dinner with myself... I can't cancel that again!"

"Seven o'clock: Wrestle my self-loathing...I'm booked!"

this page:
The Grinch cleans out the Lou Whos' icebox.

gance to his work that we felt a responsibility to uphold," notes Boswell. "I avoided looking at the Chuck Jones cartoon because I didn't want that influencing me, and I also had to deal with the fact that humans—not animated or drawn figures with pencil necks and baseball heads—would be sitting on the couches and chairs."

The only logic these creative folks could derive from the books was that there was no logic. Sometimes a teapot looked just like a teapot, and sometimes a flower was something too wild to conjure up. The creative team on the movie was free to let their imaginations run wild within the Seussian universe, and the result is some inspired design in collaboration with illustrators Darren Dochterman (props), Robin Richesson (set decoration), and Len Morganti (cars and bicycles).

At the beginning of the project, Boswell was admittedly stumped as to what direction to take. The Lou Who house would be the first set to shoot, so she wanted to start with the furniture in the living room. She went to Michael Corenblith's office, and they perused all of the Dr. Seuss books until they discovered a similar form repeated in various books. "I saw a leg on a machine that attached to a hooflike foot, and at that moment, I knew what all the furniture would look like."

(top)
Set decorator Merideth Boswell (right) and her leadman, Tommy Samona, dressing the Lou Who kitchen.

(bottom)
Martha May Whovier's bedroom, which Boswell decorated to match Martha's nightgown.

Her favorite set turned out to be Martha May Whovier's bedroom and living room, which were "inspired by the time in grade school when my mother accidentally dropped me off to see *Kitten with a Whip*," recalls Boswell. "Martha's set deviated from most of the rules we had established in that it was more cluttered, which gave it narrative to help explain her character." Choice of props is the common way for decorators to tell a story; however, on all the

Martha May Whovier— played by Christine Baranski—in her nightgown, created by costume designer Rita Ryack.

other sets, Boswell's priorities were palette, shape, negative space, and volume. In other words, where the pottery was placed was as important to her as the pottery itself.

"I wanted Martha's bedroom to look like a winter wonderland, and this set was where I worked closest with Rita Ryack, the costume designer. I literally built the bedroom around Martha's nightgown, and in the living room, we matched the upholstery fabric to the skirt she wears when being interviewed by Cindy." The dining room chairs and sofa in Martha's house were full Seuss versions of the miniature furniture that is made from beer cans and which is very similar to some Southern folk art.

When everyone was still getting their bearings with regard to how Seussian to make the props, Ferry came up with a criterion: A prop needed to sit in your hand like it was functional. If it couldn't, it was probably too fantastical.

Ferry and her staff frequented swap meets and antique shops and bought any item that struck their fancy. These items were then placed in the ort—or scraps closet—possibly to be used at a later time. "This was not a Velcro world we were creating, so I kept getting drawn to materials from the 1930s and '40s, like Bakelite and celluloid. The prop shop came up with a style that they coined Blizzard Deco, whereby some of the kitchen appliances looked like they were trapped in a snowdrift," says Ferry.

"The Mixmaster was perfect in that it was Seuss-like, but you immediately knew what it was," says Howard. "I felt stylistically it helped set us in the right

facing page:
Don't expect to find it at Crate & Barrel. The Grinch created his world by collecting all the things the Whos threw out over the years and kludging them together. Here is his bedroom set.

this page:
Martha May Whovier (Christine Baranski) gets set to fire the Gatling gun (created by special effects coordinator Allen Hall) that shoots Christmas lights onto her house. The effect of the lights coming out of the gun and attaching to the house was achieved by pulling the lights off the house and reversing the film.

direction." Ironically, this was a new appliance that was tweaked (with a 1950s juicer kludged onto it), but does not appear in the movie.

Here are some of the more imaginative props (there were 160, not counting duplicates) that were kludged:

- The Grinch's answering machine was made from a 1940s Kirby vacuum cleaner, a kitchen strainer, and a porcelain sink handle, among many other orts.

- Cindy's record player was based on a 1945 General Electric model, which, with its teardrop shape, had a childish feel to it. It was painted pink and white to match the color motif in the room. A spinning ballerina on top was prop shop foreman Jim Roberts' idea. The knobs were made from dental acrylic.

- Cindy's blabacorder, used for her interviews, was totally fabricated by the prop shop out of pieces from the ort room. Ferry used antique knobs, as she did for many items, and had problems getting more when she had to make duplicates. The script RCW on the machine stands for Radio Corporation of Whoville.

(left)
Mayor May Who (Jeffrey Tambor) announcing the various events the Cheermeister must preside over as part of his duties. The basis of his "microphone" is a 1930s flour sifter held in place by assorted springs.

(middle)
Cindy's blabacorder, with which she conducted her interviews, was designed to echo the feel of an old Fender amplifier.

(right)
Everything but the kitchen sink. The legs of the Grinch's telescope consist of a mannequin leg, part of an antique camera tripod, and a piece of a rain gutter. A brass sextant is found on top of the telescope.

- Used by the mayor during the Whobilation and the lighting contest, the microphone is built around a flour sifter suspended by a series of springs.

- The Grinch's oscillating razor was based on period razors, though part of it came from an animal-hair clipper.

- The Grinch's telescope was a unique combination of camera tripod leg, mannequin leg, rain gutter, and brass sextant.

Still, things bigger than props were part of the Grinch's world and of Whoville and they needed to look just right and, of equal importance, had to work. Into this breach stepped special effects coordinator Allen Hall and his crew who built the Seussy machines and the eleven Whoville vehicles. The vehicles all started with the chassis from golf carts, but it's there that any similarity with the real world ended. Of everything created for the show, the vehicles might be the most emblematic of the whimsical nature of Dr. Seuss. Hall's crew took between two and four

(left)
The Grinch spies on the festivities in Whoville. The Whos' cheer and goodwill are more than the Grinch can bear.

(insets, right)
Darren Dochterman's sketch of the blabacorder and Robin Richesson's drawings of some of the furnishings from the Lou Who house.

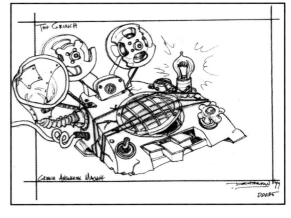

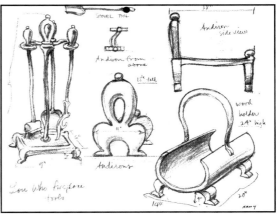

facing page:
Orts R Us. The Grinch checks his ever-shrinking heart on the X-ray machine made from leftover machine parts. Although this scene was cut from the movie, the blue screen was inserted so that a digital artist could create an animated composite of the Grinch's heart and rib cage.

this page:
The cars, designed from golf carts by Allen Hall, proved irresistible to the crew. Ron Howard takes a test drive. Nine cars were created from scratch and now reside at Universal Studios' theme parks in Hollywood and Orlando. The vehicle sketches are by Len Morganti.

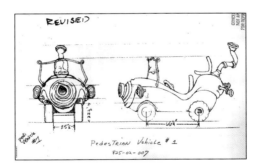

weeks to sculpt a car's body from foam, another two weeks to make a mold, two to three more weeks assembling the vehicle, and then one week giving it a lustrous paint job. Those who had work to do during off-hours or on weekends were unable to refrain from touring around Whoville, usually in the convertible roadster.

Laugh Now, but Wait Until It's Selling on Melrose Avenue

"I was terrified," says costume designer Rita Ryack upon finding out she would be the designer for the movie. "I started as an animator and cartoonist, so Dr. Seuss was this revered and venerated influence, and so this movie became a terrible responsibility. I actually had a thought—briefly—that maybe I shouldn't do it."

Prior to starting on the movie, Ryack was lecturing at a seminar for film students at New York University, where she asked her startled students, "I'm about to start *Dr. Seuss' How the Grinch Stole Christmas!* and does anybody here have any ideas?" She adds, "It's rather strange, but I felt such pressure because he [Geisel] had the most original voice."

this page:
Martha May reacts to seeing the Grinch again after all these years.

facing page:
Having accepted the invitation of the Whos to be Wholiday Cheermeister, the Grinch is horrified when he sees the sweater that he has been forced to don. Covering his entire eyeball, the yellow contact lenses were a constant irritation. Despite his discomfort at "being buried alive" beneath the makeup, lenses, and costume, Carrey felt perfectly at ease the minute Howard called "Action!"

Costume designer Rita Ryack puts the finishing touches on extra William Scudder.

The last leg of the creative relay team to join the sprint toward production, Ryack began work in May 1999 knowing she had to come up with more than four hundred outfits and two hundred hats for a movie, the filming of which was to begin in four short months. Ryack locked herself at home and frenetically tried to draw like Dr. Seuss, hoping "that eventually I would channel him." Ryack would come to Ron Howard's office on the Universal lot with an armful of sketches on napkins, on the margins of memos, paper bags, and sometimes even sketching paper. Ryack would add her own dialogue to sketches, not as a suggestion but rather to help herself in the creative process. More often than not, she and Howard agreed on the direction of the costumes and even toyed with the idea of adding tails to the Whos, inspired by the 1954 Dr. Seuss book *Horton Hears a Who!* Eventually, the major work came during the test fittings with the actors when Ryack was able to see how the actors could move in the costumes.

Ryack started trial sketches of the Whos based on **Horton Hears a Who!** Like Rick Baker, she was faced with the problem of making the Whos **in the spirit** of Dr. Seuss without making them too cute or clownlike. Ryack finally found her way, through sketches of hats. "His books are always full of hats," she notes. Fittingly, the movie has some of the wildest hats imaginable. The inspiration for them sprang from a most unlikely source.

"I got a lot of inspiration from 1950s cookbooks, which were styled just so and had wonderful **National Geographic**–like colors," says Ryack, who truly did use food as a metaphor. The entire Lou Who family is adorned with assorted culinary items for Whoville's climactic Whobilation celebration.

Once she got a creative rhythm going, Ryack drew a lot of inspiration from Japanese fashion for the Who teenagers and the school uniforms for the Who children, including the young Grinch. Part hip-hop, part alternative, the look is very much that of current Japanese teen fashions. "I'm hoping that when the movie comes out, the teens' costumes will still be hip," says Ryack.

The last person to join the production team, Rita Ryack had four short months to come up with more than four hundred outfits and two hundred hats. Here are some of her sketches.

Having set the Grinch up to be humiliated at the Whobilation, Mayor May Who (Jeffrey Tambor) proposes marriage to Martha May Whovier (Christine Baranski). The outfit Tambor wore in this sequence "made me feel like I was wearing a sofa." Costume designer Rita Ryack saw the character as an amalgam of the mayor from Dr. Seuss' *And to Think That I Saw It on Mulberry Street* and the Monopoly man from the board game.

Lacey Kohl plays the one Who who has a certain sex appeal, although the makeup and the padding around her midsection don't exactly inspire thoughts of classical beauty. For the Whobilation, Ryack outfitted her and Nadja Poinilla in candy cane outfits inspired by Las Vegas showgirls.

"Inspire" is the key word here, because nothing used in the movie could be bought. It all had to be designed and built from scratch, starting with the shoes. The tailors assigned to the project had to work against their natural instinct to flatter the human body by minimizing the waistlines and broadening the shoulders. Instead, they had to stitch clothing around pear-shaped lower-torso padding and soft, sloping shoulders. "People love puppies because they have big feet, big eyes, and are a little chubby and basically out of proportion. To make lovable-looking Whos out of the actors, we had to play against the [expected human] proportions and make them a little more androgynous," notes Ryack of the endomorphic model. And because of the look, the actors' carriage and stride were dramatically affected.

(left)
At the beginning of the movie, the Lou Who boys are egged on to approach the Grinch's cave by Lacey Kohl (right) and Nadja Poinilla, who later appear in the Whobilation sequence in candy cane outfits, inspired by the outfits of Las Vegas showgirls.

(middle)
Landry Albright plays young Martha May, who is smitten with the young Grinch. The school uniforms were inspired by old Japanese school uniforms.

(right)
Miss Rue Who, the Whoville teacher, is played by Mary Stein. Nearly six feet tall with a long, elegant neck, Mary was Rick Baker's favorite Who from a design point of view.

"Your center of gravity—to the eye, at least—is lowered, with that impossible Seussian pouch going forward and an accentuated rear end, and you waddle some because the padding makes your legs wider," says Bill Irwin, who plays Lou Who, the befuddled postmaster of Whoville. "More than the make-up, the wardrobe really transformed me into my role."

Ryack endeavored to use materials that would have been available when Dr. Seuss was writing the book. "I tried to evoke the feelings I had when I first read his books and the ambience of that time: a 1950s Norman Rockwell, television kind of world. I also wanted to remain within a kind of Technicolor palette with primary colors. In fact, for the clothes, the reds and the greens became neutrals." (Because of the on-set blue screen, necessitated by subsequent visual effects shots, blue does not exist, nor do the colors purple or magenta, the latter two being personal nonpreferences of Ryack's, anyway.)

The Rockwell model served for her designs for the Lou Who family, which Ryack outfitted as a cockeyed version of the perfect television family. For the scene in which the pajama-clad Whos congregate in the town square the

It's alive! Having never laid eyes on the Grinch, all of Whoville recoils in horror at the first word they hear him utter: "Boo!" The blue screen behind the actors is a blank canvas upon which the visual effects team will later project computer-generated Whos.

morning after Christmas has been stolen, Ryack resorted to 1950s patterns for nearly all her creations. The outfits for Betty Lou Who—Molly Shannon—were straight out of a 1950s television sitcom. They evolved from very frumpy to something a little more pleasing to the eye, at Ron Howard's request.

If the costume design seems like children playing dress-up with dolls, that is not too far from the reality of the movie. Never was the motif more fully realized than when Ryack created the wardrobe for Martha May Whovier, played by Christine Baranski.

"I never had a Barbie of my own," notes Ryack, "but I sure got to design a movie star Barbie, because Christine really knows how to work a costume."

"I have never worn clothes as dazzling as this character's. They're like couture clothes in the extreme," notes Baranski. "Exaggeratedly beautiful and elegant."

One day on the large Whoville set amidst a couple hundred cast and crew, first assistant director Aldric Porter was looking around for Baranski, who called out to him. Seeing Baranski in a party gown that was, whether by virtue of the actress or the costume, glittering, Porter responded, "Ah, Christine! Why don't you float on over to the camera?"

"I originally pictured Martha as Waspy and sort of sleek," recalls Ryack, "but when she got her hair and makeup, her character was more like Eva Gabor. Still, I was very pleased with the way [her costume] worked out."

Jeffrey Tambor's character, Mayor May Who, is an amalgam of the mayor from Dr. Seuss' first book **And to Think That I Saw It on Mulberry Street** and the Monopoly man from the board game. The outfit he wore to the Whobilation festivities made Tambor feel "like I was wearing a sofa." The mayor's silhouette is the reverse of everyone else's. While everyone else is pear-shaped, May Who is corseted with a padded chest and big shoulders, all adding to the desired image of sheer pomposity. May Who's sidekick, the sycophantic Who Bris, played by Ron's brother, Clint Howard, has a more cartoonish look, inspired by 1950s **Mad** magazines.

Whether because of her desire to "channel" Seuss, her attempt to evoke the childhood feeling of reading Seuss, or maybe even sheer lack of time, Ryack enlisted the help of the second-grade class of one of her colleague's sons. "I wanted to have a child's point of view, so I gave Ed Hanley's son's class a lot of craft materials—glitter, cardboard, Popsicle sticks—and they made presents and stars. I used a lot of that stuff to help decorate some of the children's outfits. You see, Whobilation is like Mardi Gras for the Whos, so you really can't go too overboard when it comes to what they're wearing."

facing page:
(top)
Christine Baranski's Martha May Whovier, the Aphrodite of the Whos. In her world, aesthetic considerations took precedence over all else. Her negligee matched her linens, which matched the lampshades. At one point during the numerous makeup tests, there was talk that Baranski might not even need a prosthetic nosepiece since, as she herself put it, "I have a God-given Who nose."

(bottom)
The Lou Whos in Ryack's food-inspired outfits.

this page:
(top)
A wary Mayor May Who (Jeffrey Tambor) emerges from the Whoville grocery store after hearing about a Grinch "sighting." May Who is the traditionalist who wants each Christmas to be a little better and bigger than the one before.

(bottom)
Because Taylor Momsen (right) as a minor could work only limited hours, it was necessary to find an adult double. There was lots of stunt work for the character, but finding someone Taylor's size (forty-two inches tall and forty pounds) was not easy. After failing to find anyone locally, stunt coordinator Charlie Croughwell tried little people's organizations as well as circuses across the country. Finally, in a circus in Russia, he tracked down Oxana Nenakhova (left), a star performer earning $40 *a month*. As a SAG performer, she made a *weekly* salary of $2,222, not counting overtime or stunt adjustments.

Chuck Jones Never Had It This Complicated

After his literal change of heart, the Grinch realizes the sleigh is about to fall off the top of Mt. Crumpit — with all the presents—and he actually cares. The blue screen behind the Grinch was replaced with the surrounding Whoville mountain range and sky, created by the visual effects production company Digital Domain. Led by the movie's visual effects supervisor Kevin Mack, the company created about 350 shots that encompassed set extensions for existing filmed shots, computer-generated Whos to augment certain Whoville scenes, and scenes entirely computer-generated, such as the opening of the movie.

It's polite to argue otherwise, but the movie business, at its core, has always been about only two things: the creation of material and its interpretation. Decisions about these things are made by the actor, writer, director, and producer—the same folks who get the long-term deals at the studios. Everyone else on a movie set is in service of that quartet and is either perfectly content with their job or hopes one day to be among that elite band. Ron Howard's productions are unique in that he welcomes and even encourages input on creative matters from his crew.

Howard doesn't do this to be polite (which he unfailingly is); rather, he does it in his continual quest to avoid working in a vacuum. "Ron always wants to know what others are thinking," says his longtime associate producer, Louisa Velis. "When his dad suggests something and his wife suggests something, he takes into consideration that they're coming from different perspectives. Once he knows someone's personality—where they are coming from—he carefully considers their input."

One month after wrapping on the film, Howard invited the production office staff and the accounting department to a screening. Delighted to be included, since they were rarely on the set or in dailies, they were downright flabbergasted the next morning when Howard assembled them for an hour-long session and asked them what they thought of the movie and whether they had any suggestions.

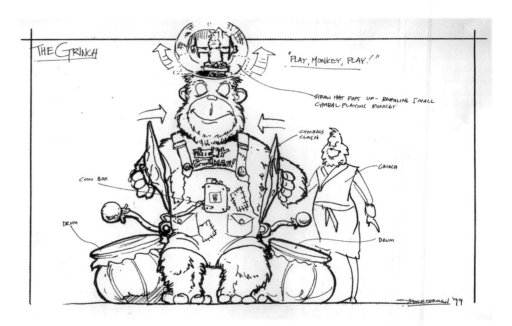

Kids, don't try this at home. The crescendo of cheers emanating from Whoville has compelled the Grinch to resort to extreme methods to drive the sound from his head. Built by Allen Hall, the monkey's giant cymbals had to be operated manually here by Joe Montenegro because the mechanized force would have fractured Jim Carrey's skull. Don Peterman (on stepladder) uses a flashlight to augment the lighting.

A longtime associate of Howard's—first as a production designer and now as executive producer and second unit director—Todd Hallowell used storyboard artists Peter Ramsey, Eric Ramsey, and Tom McGrath to visually plot out the script pages. The four would get together a couple times a week and go over the storyboards. Out of these sessions came some ideas for scenes or gags not in the script. During one such session, they were trying to dream up some loud and annoying business for the Grinch in his cave to drown out the singing drifting up from Whoville. Hallowell came up with the Grinch hopping around the cave on a jackhammer, and Eric Ramsey came up with the idea of the classic mechanical monkey (bobbing head, clapping cymbals)—except this one would be ten feet tall. Special effects coordinator Allen Hall took the twelve-inch version, scaled it up, and installed a motor. In the scene where the Grinch has his head between the cymbals as Cindy approaches him, the effects crew had to move the monkey's arms manually because the motor-driven arms would have fractured Jim Carrey's skull.

Such a contagious atmosphere of creativity is exemplified when Hallowell gave his marching orders to his storyboard artists: "The Grinch has to flee Whoville, so let's come up with some ways for him to make his escape." McGrath came up with the idea of the Grinch appropriating a tiny car belonging to tiny Whos as his means of escape. A modest idea on paper (so were World War II movies, with the stage direction EXT. BEACH: The Allies invade Normandy) helped build entire scenes before and after it, which entailed both shooting units and all the departments involved with the movie.

This sequence is also representative of how visual effects integrated itself into all areas of production. Digital Domain, the company that created and won Academy Awards for the visual effects for *Titanic* and *What Dreams May Come*, was assigned the task of extending and amplifying the world of

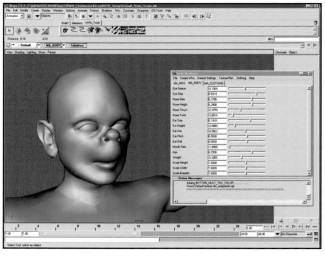

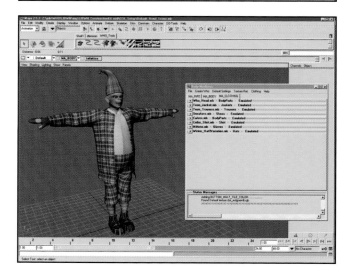

8 6

facing page:
(left-hand column)
Utilizing varying combinations of costumes and facial and body features, Digital Domain's proprietary software could generate an infinite variety of Whos.

(right-hand column)
Mayor May Who reassures the Whos that there is no Grinch problem in Whoville. On a set of such hugeness, one hundred actors are not sufficient to make a convincing crowd scene. In the bottom shot, Digital Domain used computer-generated Whos to fill out the frame. Extensions beyond the physically constructed set give Whoville greater depth. The computer-generated Whos were based on Rick Baker's faces and Rita Ryack's wardrobe designs and were animated as well. What made this shot so complicated was that some of the computer-generated Whos have been added in the foreground, requiring painstaking detail. When the computer-generated Whos are in the background, they can be more rudimentary in texture and animation (top right).

this page:
The topography of Whoville needed to be created. Where did it lie in relation to Mt. Crumpit? And where did Mt. Crumpit lie in relation to its surroundings? How realistic or how fanciful should it look? A wire-frame rendering of the area in 3-D (top) was the first step and it was then further rendered with texture and color (below). Mt. Crumpit is the peak in the right foreground.

Whoville. Digital Domain's proprietary software, in conjunction with Rick Baker's makeup design and Rita Ryack's costume design, gave rise to scores of original Whos. Digital Domain did a cyberscan of some of Baker's prosthetic rubber appliances, which yielded 3-D models of assorted Whos. The life cast of the Grinch was also scanned so that Digital could insert the Grinch into parts of the harrowing sleigh-ride sequence.

Whoville was extended beyond the mere physical boundaries established by the film unit as additional buildings were computer-generated, creating an entire city nestled in a mountain valley in the shadow of Mt. Crumpit. Again, close collaboration among production designer Michael Corenblith, art director Dan Webster (who oversaw the color palette), visual effects producer Kurt Williams, Digital Domain's Kevin Mack (the usual effects supervisor), and Julian Levi (visual effects producer) was essential to the seamless integration of the two separate production units. Well over four hundred shots were computer-generated for the movie, and all had to dovetail into existing shots from production.

Once the Grinch concludes that the Whos and their Whobilation represent everything that is wrong with Christmas, he decides that his duties as Wholiday Cheermeister include burning down the Christmas tree, which sets

this page:
A moving camera platform driven by stunt coordinator Charlie Croughwell (seated on left), with a limber Jim Carrey having folded himself on top of the tiny Who car.

facing page:
The Grinch is foiled in his attempt to hide from Cindy in the Post Office when Max sneezes and gives them away. The top photo shows the scene as shot with the blue screen ceiling above Carrey's head. The bottom photo shows another shot in the same sequence. The ceiling extension created by Digital Domain adds a touch of Seussian architectural whimsy.

off pandemonium—a set of affairs tailor-made to Jim Carrey's improvisational talents. "So much of production is managing your compromises," notes Howard. "Except in the case of a movie like this, where a character so excels and so exceeds whatever expectations. In the tough hours of managing this movie, Jim's performance and creativity always buoyed me."

As the tree is burning, the Grinch exclaims, "Oh, the Whomanity!" (à la the audio report from the *Hindenburg* disaster). When the Grinch tries to hail a

taxi as a getaway car and the taxi refuses to stop for him, he cries out, "It's because I'm green, isn't it?" (At the time of the shoot, actor Danny Glover was in the news when he said that New York City cabdrivers would not pick him up because he is black.) And finally, as Carrey scoots around Whoville on a self-propelled car appropriated from the tiny Whos, he proclaims, "Eat my dust!" (a reference to the 1976 movie of the same name Ron Howard starred in). "That scene was fun, but I could barely keep my balance on that thing," recalls Carrey. The tiny Who car sequence was directed by both Howard and Hallowell's second unit, with Hallowell coming up with a subtle homage to *Battleship Potemkin* as the Grinch narrowly misses a Who and her baby carriage.

Ron Howard sets Jim Carrey in position to stop the tiny Who car. The car is painted blue so a shot of real-sized actors Caroline Williams and John Short in a regular-sized Who car—seen from the Grinch's point of view—could be composited into the shot. Second unit director Todd Hallowell did the shot of the tiny Whos on a separate day.

Stunt coordinator Charlie Croughwell created a rig—using the extended base of a wheelchair—so that he could drive Jim Carrey—seated on the tiny Who car—all over Whoville. A flying rig, attached to the perms on Stage 12, consisted of an I-beam, which allowed Croughwell to spin the car around and around and then permitted Grinch stunt double Pat Banta to travel twenty-five feet through the air and ten feet off the ground. Throughout this car chase, the Grinch narrowly misses assorted Whos and sends them tumbling. These stunt people—Sonny Tipton, Terry Notary, Greg Wise, Fricso Canyon, Richie Gaona, Stas Greiner, Svetla Krasteva, and Pavel Soukharev—came from the Las Vegas–based troupe of the *Mystère* show of Cirque du Soleil. "The Cirque performers have a strong performance background doing odd characters in odd situations, so they were perfect for the movie," says Croughwell. "There are not too many stunt people I could find who I could ask to climb up

A good example of the work Digital Domain did in creating a mood is exemplified in the scene of the Grinch bellowing his individual dislike of the Whoville residents. The top photo shows the scene as filmed on Stage 27 with the lights, the blue screen, and the ceiling visible. In the center photograph, an ominous sky has been added. In the bottom shot, breath from the Grinch's mouth and flying snow complete the shot.

a pole upside down only with their hands. These guys give you a broad range of abilities that you normally don't get."

Prior to production, Croughwell coordinated three weeks of "Who School" for the actors and stunt performers, during which they developed a body language for the Whos. How far can the Whos defy gravity? What can Whos do that normal people cannot do? "Sometimes, Seuss would show Whos defying the laws of physics, standing on their toe on the corner of a box, on top of a pile of boxes balanced on their corners, all while playing badminton. Other times, they were like normal people," notes Croughwell.

And so it went…wrestling the whimsical world of Dr. Seuss from two dimensions into three—while being true to the unique logic of his universe and to his sensibilities. And all along, probably firmly lodged in all these talented minds was the notion that Dr. Seuss had helped them learn to read when they were children and that, therefore, a large responsibility had been conferred upon them. Michael Corenblith best summed it up when he said: "When I realized what I had to live up to, I thought, 'Please don't screw this up.'"

Filming the ring of Whos and
the Grinch singing "Welcome,
Christmas" around the
Whoville Christmas tree.
More computer-generated
Whos were added later.